Monk

"I'm surrounded by crocodiles!" shouted the Professor.

The crocodiles were getting closer now and one of them started to clamber up on to the island, directly behind the place where the Professor was standing.

"Look out!" shouted George, waving his arms up and down to attract the Professor's attention. "Look out behind you!"

The Professor spun round. The great crocodile was now very close to him, its eyes fixed intently on what it thought would be its next meal. With a yell of alarm, the Professor dashed towards the closest of the island's two trees and clambered up on to a branch.

He was just in time.

Best wishes,

Alexander McCall Smith

More exciting adventure stories from
Alexander McCall Smith!

ALEXANDER McCALL SMITH

Monkey Boy

Illustrated by Tania Hurt-Newton

To Pier-Carlo Cadoppi

Scholastic Children's Books,
Commonwealth House, 1-19 New Oxford Street,
London WC1A 1NU, UK
a division of Scholastic Ltd
London ~ New York ~ Toronto ~ Sydney ~ Auckland
Mexico City ~ New Delhi ~ Hong Kong

Published in the UK by Scholastic Ltd, 2000

ISBN 0 439 01332 1

Printed by Cox & Wyman Ltd, Reading, Berks.

10 9 8 7 6 5 4 3 2 1

Chapter 1

A Very Peculiar Thing

I know that some of you are not going to believe this. Yet there are some very strange things that are quite true, and this is one of them.

This is a picture of George. As you can see, he looks like any other boy. He's wearing the same sort of things that most boys wear. His hair is a bit untidy, it must be said, and he has a few freckles on the end of his nose. But if you take a closer look, you may notice something odd. George looks rather like a monkey.

Perhaps it's because of his longer than usual arms. They go down almost to his knees. And his hands, you will have noticed, turn in a bit, rather like a monkey's. And when it comes to his face – now that you come to mention it – it does remind one a little bit of a monkey's face.

"George is a rather strange child," his mother remarked one day. "Have you thought about the way he walks?"

George's father looked thoughtful.

"Yes," he said. "I've often wondered why he swings his arms from side to side. Do other boys do that?"

"No," said his mother. "I don't think they do. Only George."

After that, George's father watched his son a bit more closely, and he began to notice other unusual things. He noticed how good George was at climbing trees. No tree was too tall or too slippery for George. Up he went, hauling himself up the trunk and into the branches as if it were the easiest thing in the world.

"Look at George!" his friends shouted when they went on the school picnic. "He's up a tree!"

"George!" shouted the teacher. "What are you doing up there? Come down here this moment!"

But George did not hear the teacher. He was up in the highest branches of the tallest tree in the field, and he was having the time of his life! Holding on with his rather long arms, George swung from branch to branch, moving in and out through the leaves – it was a breathtaking sight.

"There he is!" the others cried. "Look at him swing!"

While the others ate their picnic down on the ground, George took a banana from his pocket and ate it. Then, when he had finished, he hung down from one of the branches by his feet and dangled the banana skin over his best friend's head.

That made everybody laugh, including the teacher, who had now realized that George was perfectly safe up in the tree and had stopped trying to get him down.

"That boy was just like a monkey," the teacher remarked later. "If you put him in the zoo, you wouldn't know the difference."

The teacher had meant that as a joke, but it turned out that what she said was really quite true. Some months later, as its school treat, George's class was taken to the zoo, and there a very peculiar thing happened.

It was just after they had arrived and had started to look at the animals. They had seen the lions, who had not yet been given their lunch and who were feeling rather hungry.

The lions looked at the class and licked their lips, wondering which of the children they would like to eat first – if they had the chance. Then they had gone on to look at some kangaroos, which had kindly given a few demonstration bounces. After that, they went on to the monkey house, and this is where the trouble started.

The monkeys lived in a large, sunken pen, which was open to the sky. It had several tall trees in it and was full of ferns and bushes to make the monkeys feel at home. Around the edge of their pen there was a wall, over which you could lean and look down at what was happening below.

Everybody was busy looking at the monkeys when, quite without warning,

George toppled over the edge and fell down into the pen below. The teacher gave a shriek when she realized what had happened, but fortunately George's fall was broken by a bush and he was quite unhurt.

"George!" shouted the teacher. "Stay exactly where you are. I'll go to fetch help."

George looked about him. He was very close to a large tree, and he thought that if he climbed up that he would be able to clamber along a branch and get out of the pen that way.

"I'm all right," he shouted up to his friends. "I can climb out on my own."

George found no difficulty climbing up the tree-trunk and was soon resting on a branch. It was while he was there, and before he had time to do anything else, that he realized that he was not alone in the tree. There, at the other end of the branch, several large monkeys were sitting, staring at him suspiciously.

George felt in his pocket. As usual, he had brought a banana with him, and he now took this out, peeled it, and handed it to the largest of the monkeys.

The monkey snatched the banana from him, inspected it, and then crammed it into his mouth before the others had time to claim their share.

"Sorry," said George. "I only brought one."

The other monkeys seemed to understand this, and they edged gingerly along the branch until they were sitting right next to George. Then they began to run their little monkey fingers through his hair, as monkeys like to do. George did not mind this at all, and he did the same for them. It was all very comfortable, sitting up on the branch with his new friends, while all his old friends stood on the other side of the wall and looked up in astonishment.

In the meantime, the teacher had arrived back with one of the zoo-keepers, who was carrying a ladder.

"There he is," she said, pointing up at the branch. The zoo-keeper shaded his eyes from the sun and looked up into the tree.

"Where?" he asked. "Are you sure he's up there?"

"I think so," said the teacher. "At least, I thought I saw him."

"Those are monkeys up there," said the zoo-keeper. "I don't see any boy."

The teacher stared hard.

"George?" she shouted. "Is that you up there on that branch?"

George looked down and waved. And then, without further ado, he swung along the branch, hand over hand, followed by his new monkey friends.

"There he is," shouted a member of the class. "That's him."

The zoo-keeper was astonished.

He had never before seen a boy move through the trees exactly like a monkey, and he was quite open-mouthed with disbelief by the time that George eventually lowered himself from the end of the branch, waved a cheerful goodbye to the monkeys, and came to report to the teacher.

"This has been a most remarkable incident," the zoo-keeper said. "I hope you don't mind if I tell the newspapers all about it. They are always on the look-out for a good zoo story."

George did not mind. Nor did he mind when his photograph was published the following day.

"Monkey Boy Saved By Monkeys!" ran the newspaper headline. "George O'Tang, a local schoolboy, yesterday astonished everybody at the zoo when he fell into the monkey enclosure and was brought out by a pack of monkeys."

Of course this was not strictly true. The monkeys had not actually saved George. He had really saved himself, but the rest of the story was true enough.

George thought nothing more about it.

But that day, quite by chance, the newspaper was picked up by a famous professor who happened to be visiting the town. This professor, who was called Professor Frederick J. Dodd, was one of the world's great experts on monkeys. He examined the picture of George with interest and noted down the details in his notebook. George did not know it at the time, but a great adventure was about to begin!

Chapter 2

The Professor's Plan

The next evening George's father answered a knock on the door. There, standing on the front doorstep, was Professor Frederick J. Dodd, and in his hand was a copy of yesterday's newspaper.

"I take it that this is the house of George O'Tang," said the Professor, in a courteous voice. "And you, sir, I take to be George's father."

Mr O'Tang nodded. He wondered whether George had got into trouble of some sort and whether their visitor had come to complain about his swinging through his garden or something like that. But the Professor did not look like somebody who had come to complain. In fact, he looked quite friendly.

So George's father invited the Professor in and they were soon sitting in the living room, with the Professor still smiling broadly and looking about him in an interested sort of way.

"I am Professor Frederick J. Dodd," the Professor began. "I am a person who studies monkeys. In fact, I am the Director of the Institute of Monkeyology, which, as you know, is all about the study of monkeys."

"I'm afraid I didn't know that," confessed Mr O'Tang. "But I'm sure that's a very interesting thing to do."

The Professor beamed with pleasure.

"Oh it is, sir," he said. "And at this very moment I am engaged in a fascinating study of monkeys in the jungles of the Congo, which, as you know is in the middle of Africa."

George's father smiled politely. He wondered what all this had to do with him. He knew that his son looked like a monkey, and often behaved like one, but surely the Professor could not seriously be thinking of studying George.

"I shall get to the point," said the Professor. "The study that I am carrying out is in trouble. The monkeys I am studying are very rare. In fact, there are only one hundred of them left in the whole of Africa. They are also very shy, and something is disturbing them. I need somebody to help me to find out what it is."

"I see," said George's father. "I would like to help you, but I'm afraid that I can't really get away to Africa. I have to go to work every day, you see. I'm just too busy."

The Professor laughed.

"I wasn't thinking of you," he said after a moment. "I was thinking of your son, George, the one in the newspaper."

Mr O'Tang gasped.

"Do you mean that you want my son George to go off to the jungles of the Congo?"

"Yes," said the Professor, smiling.

"He is exactly the sort of boy I need. He can climb, you see, and. . ." The Professor hesitated before going on. "And he does look remarkably like a monkey. I don't mean to give offence or anything like that, of course. As far as I'm concerned, it's a wonderful thing to look like a monkey. Monkeys are so interesting, you see."

George's father was silent for a moment. It was surely a very dangerous thing to go off to the jungles of the Congo, but he was a kind man and he liked monkeys. Also, deep inside him, he was proud of the fact that he had such an unusual son, and he would not want to stop him having an adventure – if one ever came along.

"Very well," he said at last. "George can go along. But only if he wants to."

It was at this point that a voice shouted from outside the living room door. George had been hanging upside-down from the stairs above and had heard every word that the Professor had said.

"Of course I want to go," he shouted. "When will we be leaving?"

"Tomorrow?" shouted the Professor in the direction of the voice. "Will that give you enough time to get ready?"

George gave a yelp of delight and went straight off to his room to begin packing. Africa! The Congo! It was almost too exciting to believe.

Chapter 3

In the Congo

It was a long journey to Africa. The Institute of Monkeyology had its own plane, a rather old one which could not fly very fast – or very high. George helped to read the map, as the pilot was rather short-sighted and found it difficult to see exactly where they were. But at last they arrived, and George saw the little landing-strip down below them, on the edge of the great river which snaked its way through the jungle.

"There!" he shouted. "There it is!"

The pilot and the Professor both peered out of the plane, but could see nothing.

"Turn right," shouted George. "Then go a little bit to the left and a little bit lower."

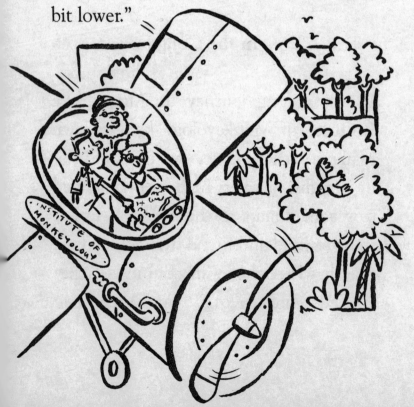

The pilot did as he was told, and at last, just as they were right above the tops of the trees, he saw the landing strip and brought the plane down with a bump.

George and the Professor unloaded their trunks and crates of equipment. Then they said goodbye to the pilot, who promised to come back to collect them in four days, and began to set up camp.

The Professor had thought of everything. There were comfortable camp beds with blow-up air mattresses and blow-up air pillows. There were nets to hang over the beds to keep out the bugs, and there were hooks on which to hang your shoes.

"It's most important to hang your shoes up when you're in the jungle," the Professor explained. "If you leave them under your bed overnight then all sorts of things get into them and you get a nasty surprise when you put them on in the morning. I once put my foot into my shoe and got a nasty bite from a Kilimanjaro Toe-Biter."

George shuddered. A Kilimanjaro Toe-Biter? What could that be?

"A snake," said the Professor, reading his mind. "It specializes in biting toes and I can assure you its bites are very, very sore."

By the time that night fell, the camp was entirely prepared. The Professor had made a fire and sausages were sizzling away in a frying pan. Their tents were set up, and their monkey-studying equipment – cameras, microphones and notebooks – was all carefully laid out on a folding table. All that remained to do was to have dinner, brush their teeth at the edge of the river, and then blow out the lanterns and go to bed.

After their meal, while the Professor put more wood on the fire to keep it burning through the night, George made his way by torchlight down the path that led to the river. He had his toothbrush with him, and he had already squeezed the toothpaste on to it. It was most exciting, he thought, going to brush one's teeth in the River Congo – much more exciting than going into the bathroom at home.

He came to the edge of the river and flashed his torch out across the water. It was wide there and the beam was too weak to reach the other side, but George knew that there was nothing but jungle there anyway. He leaned forward and dipped his brush into the water, and it was at that moment that he heard a shout behind him. It was the Professor's voice, but George could not make out what he was trying to say. Perhaps he needed help with the fire. Well, George would help him, but he would have to finish brushing his teeth first. He bent forward again, and then he heard another shout.

George straightened up. What was the Professor going on about? It was most annoying being interrupted in this way. Perhaps he should go back up the bank of the river to see if he could make out what the shouts were about.

He took a few steps back. Now the shouting was clearer.

"Remember to be careful of crocodiles," shouted the Professor. "I forgot to tell you."

And at that point, just as George stepped back, a great crocodile, which had been lurking in the shallow water watching him, leaped out to the place where George had been standing a few seconds before. It opened its great jaws and then snapped them shut again, expecting to find a tasty morsel in its mouth. But all it tasted was air!

George watched in horror as the powerful reptile, disappointed by its failure to catch him, slid back into the water and disappeared in the current.

He decided that he would not clean his
teeth that night. It was probably better to
go to bed with dirty teeth, he thought,
than to go to bed in the stomach of a
great crocodile.

The Professor was very alarmed to hear what had happened, but was relieved that it had all turned out well.

"Those crocodiles are a dreadful nuisance," he said. "I can't tell you how many times they've tried to get me. So far, they've failed, but one never knows. . ."

They said goodnight to one another and George went off to his tent. It felt warm and safe inside, and he drifted off to sleep thinking how grand it was to be in the middle of the Congo and how exciting the next day would be. He slept well, although now and then he heard noises in the night, rustlings and squeaks. But these were nothing to worry about, he thought, as the jungle was always full of sounds.

Chapter 4

Monkey Business

When George woke up the next morning the Professor was already up and about. George heard breakfast being made and dressed quickly as the delicious smell of fried eggs and beans came drifting into his tent. He put on his clothes and was just reaching for his shoes under the bed when he remembered. His shoes were not there, of course, but were on the hook that the Professor had knocked into the tree-trunk outside.

George walked out in his bare feet and reached for his shoes. He put one shoe on and had started to put his other foot into the shoe when he gave a great yell.

The Professor, who was putting the fried eggs on to the plates, turned round sharply.

"What on earth is happening?" he cried out. "Is there something wrong?"

George had extracted his foot from the shoe in record time and was now hopping about on his other foot.

"A Kilimanjaro Toe-Biter!" he yelled. "There's one in my shoe. I felt it."

The Professor came running over. He had snatched a hammer from the folding table and when he reached

George he struck the shoe several sharp blows.

"Take that!" he shouted. "And that!"

He stopped, and they both looked at the shoe. George had expected a rather battered snake to come crawling out of it, but there was nothing. Gingerly the Professor took the shoe and tipped it up. Out of the shoe there came not a snake, nor a tarantula, nor anything like that. In fact, all that came out was a squashed banana.

43

George looked at the Professor, who suddenly burst out laughing.

"So that's what you felt," he said. "Still, I don't blame you for getting such a fright. A banana must feel very much like a snake when you can't see it."

"But how did a banana get into my shoe?" George asked.

The Professor scratched his head.

"I have no idea," he said. "Unless. . ."

He paused, looking towards the edge of the jungle. Was there a slight movement in the tops of the trees? Could it be?

"I suspect that we had a visit from the monkeys during the night," he said, his voice dropping to a whisper. "In fact, I shouldn't be surprised if they were watching us right at this moment!"

George followed the Professor's gaze.

Yes, he was sure that the Professor was right. A branch had moved, and he had seen a sudden flash of white amidst the green. There were monkeys there – he was sure of it.

Over breakfast, the Professor told George all about the monkeys they were going to study.

"This is a very unusual group of monkeys," he said. "As I mentioned the other day, they are very rare. But not only that, they are very much more intelligent than most other monkeys. Monkeys are our cousins, you see, and they are cleverer than most animals. Some of them can use simple tools – things like sticks and stones – and some of them can even be taught to switch on lights and open doors. But these monkeys, the Congo Stripy Monkeys as they are called, are even cleverer than that."

The Professor paused while he put a piece of fried egg on to a slice of bread and then popped it into his mouth.

"Mmm," he went on. "Very nice. Now as I was saying, these monkeys are very clever. In fact they are so clever that I believe that they have even worked out a special monkey writing. We know that some animals can talk to one another – whales and birds sing messages to one another – but no animal has ever been seen to write. Yet I think these monkeys may be able to do just that!"

George listened open-mouthed.

"But how do you know?" he asked. "Have you seen them do it?"

The Professor shook his head.

"I have never been able to get very close to them," he said, his voice sounding rather sad. "But I have found what look like little notes on leaves lying on the jungle floor. I think the monkeys wrote them. I would love to have more evidence."

The Professor looked thoughtful.

"Now," he went on. "This is where you come in. I believe that these monkeys will trust you and allow you to get to know them. That's because you can climb trees so well and also because. . ."

"Because?" prompted George.

"Well," said the Professor. "I don't want to hurt your feelings, but has anybody ever told you how like a monkey you look?"

George laughed. "Of course they have," he said. "And I don't mind in the slightest. After all, what's wrong with looking like a monkey? Monkeys never complain about the way they look."

"Exactly," said the Professor, feeling relieved that George had taken it so well. "Those are my feelings exactly. But now, let's finish breakfast and get down to work. We have a great deal to do today."

* * *

The Professor's plan was quite simple. They had brought with them a large supply of bananas and George was to take a pile of these to the edge of the jungle and sit beside it. Monkeys can't resist bananas, no matter how hard they try, and sooner or later the more adventurous of them would show themselves. When that happened, George was to hold out a peeled banana and let a monkey take it from him. Then, holding more bananas in one hand, he was to follow the monkeys up into the trees. In this way, they would get used to him and allow him to photograph them for the Professor.

George thought that it was a very good plan, and without further delay he began to unpack bananas from the crate. Then, with a large bunch of the delicious-smelling fruit under his arm, he sauntered over to the edge of the jungle and sat down on a tuft of grass.

For a while nothing happened. Some birds flew overhead and there were several splashes and squelches as a hippopotamus ambled into the river. But nothing seemed to be happening in the jungle itself.

After an hour or two, George began to wonder whether the monkeys had gone away, or whether they had ever really been there in the first place, but then he noticed something happening. One of the lower branches of a nearby tree was beginning to move, as if a weight was being put on it. George strained his eyes, and at last he saw it. There was a monkey, a large monkey with splendid black-and-white striped fur. Yes, there was no doubt about it. It was a Congo Stripy Monkey, and it was watching George most intently!

George pretended not to be interested. Casually he reached across to the bunch of bananas and picked one up. Then he peeled the banana, sniffed at it in a very relaxed way, and began to eat it.

"Mmm," he said softly. "What a delicious banana!"

This was too much for the monkey to bear. With a sudden bound he leaped from the branch and began to run over towards George and the bananas.

"Here," said George, in a friendly voice. "You finish it. I take it that you do like bananas?"

The monkey hesitated in his tracks. He stared at George, and then he sat still and scratched his head. He was clearly puzzled. Was this a boy or a monkey? He really wasn't sure.

"Come on," said George. "Eat it before it goes brown."

The monkey decided. This must be a monkey, he thought. No human has long arms like that and a face which looks so like a monkey's. Jumping to his feet, he bounded across to join George. George gave him the rest of the banana and then began to peel another one.

This pleased the monkey very much indeed, and he started to squeak with delight. George, who was a good mimic, also gave a squeak, and soon he and his new friend were patting one another on the back and looking for fleas in each other's hair.

After one or two more bananas, the monkey pointed towards the jungle and gave one or two more squeaks. He was obviously inviting George to join him and his friends, and so George picked up the rest of the bananas and gambolled across to the jungle, his long arms swinging in a very monkey-like way.

"Hurrah!" muttered the Professor, as he observed what was happening through his high-powered telescope. "They've accepted him straightaway. My plan is working exactly as I hoped!"

Chapter 5

At Home With the Monkeys

George decided that he would call his new friend Monkey One. The next monkey he met would be Monkey Two, and the one after that Monkey Three, and so on. In this way, he would not get mixed up when he told the Professor all about what happened.

Monkey One led him up into the same

tree from which he had jumped earlier on, and from there they moved deeper into the jungle, swinging easily from branch to branch. George found it all great fun. He had never climbed such wonderfully high trees and it all seemed very easy. Not only were the branches long and bendy, which made them ideal for swinging from, but there were also vines hanging down from the trees. These were perfect for crossing longer distances, as they made very useful swinging ropes.

After a while, they stopped, and Monkey One pointed to a taller-than-usual tree at the edge of a clearing. George looked at the tree and saw that it was teeming with Congo Stripy Monkeys, great and small. There must have been about one hundred in all, which meant that this was the entire group. Every single Congo Stripy Monkey left in this world was sitting on the one tree!

The monkeys noticed that a stranger was being brought into their midst and they stopped chattering when George and Monkey One jumped on to a branch of the great tree. Who was this new monkey? they wondered. He had no stripes at all and he was really rather big. Did Monkey One really know what he was doing, bringing a stranger along?

They climbed up to the top of the tree, where the monkeys had made a sort of platform out of twigs and leaves. There, with a wonderful view over the top of the jungle, sat three older monkeys. These, George thought were the leaders, Monkey Two, Monkey Three and Monkey Four. Monkey Four, who was the oldest, was also obviously the senior monkey. He had a marvellous coat of thick, stripy fur, and although his face sagged a little bit with age, it was full of wisdom.

Monkey Four stood up and held out a paw, which George took and shook. Then he reached for his bunch of bananas and gave one to each of the older monkeys. This was a very wise thing to do, as it is always polite to give a present when you make a visit, and this rule holds for monkeys as much as for people.

The monkeys sat and ate their bananas contentedly, all the time looking at their visitor with friendly interest. Then, just as the last morsel had been finished, there came from below the most terrible howling and wailing. Immediately George's new friends dropped the banana skins and peered down at the branches below, gesturing to George to look as well.

What George saw turned him cold with fear. Four great gorillas were stamping about at the bottom of the tree, twisting branches and grabbing at the tails of any monkey unlucky enough to be within reach. At the same time they were reaching up and snatching any food they could find – berries which the monkeys had picked in the jungle, or nuts which they had carefully stacked in the lowest branches of their home. It was a terrible sight.

The attack lasted only a few minutes, but by the time the gorillas had stamped away, the entire colony of Congo Stripys had been reduced to gibbering wrecks. George waited for a short time at the top of the tree before he decided it was safe to climb down. He now knew what it was that was worrying the monkeys and he could not wait to tell the Professor about it.

"I'll be back," he said to Monkey One. "Don't worry. And maybe I'll have some idea about how to help you."

Monkey One went with George to the edge of the jungle, just in case he should lose his way. Then he waved goodbye as George made his way back to the camp. There the Professor was waiting, eager to hear all about what had happened.

Chapter 6

The Professor's Plan

"So that's what's been troubling them!" exclaimed the Professor. "There shouldn't be gorillas in this part of the jungle. They have no business bullying the monkeys like that!"

George agreed.

"They're taking all their food," he said. "And they're pulling their tails if they get close enough."

The Professor shook his head angrily.

"If this carries on," he said, "sooner or later there'll be no Congo Stripy Monkeys left. We must do something to help them."

George racked his brains. It would not be easy to deal with a group of determined gorillas. Gorillas are large creatures, bigger and stronger than any human being, and quite capable of squashing you quite flat if you were unwise enough to get too close to them. It was hard to see what they would be able to do to help.

Then the Professor had an idea. For a moment he said nothing as he went over the idea in his mind. Then he leapt to his feet in excitement.

"I've got it," he cried out, so loudly that several parrots flew up from the tree above them, squawking in alarm. "These monkeys are very intelligent, aren't they?"

George nodded. He was sure that the monkeys he had met were every bit as intelligent as some people he knew – perhaps even a bit more.

"Well," said the Professor, calming down a little. "Let's teach them to make gorilla traps!"

George was not sure about this. If you dug a large hole and a gorilla fell into it, then all you would end up with would be a very angry gorilla who would soon find his way out. No, it did not sound like a good idea to him.

"Of course, I don't mean a trap to *catch* them," added the Professor hurriedly. "I mean traps which will drive them away, back to their own homes."

George listened as the Professor explained. It was a good idea, he had to agree – and it might just work.

"We'll try it tomorrow," said the Professor. "In the meantime, go back to your friends in the jungle and get them started on collecting the bits and pieces that we'll need. Do you think they'll understand?"

"I'm sure they will," said George.

George went back into the jungle. It was a bit difficult finding his way back to the tree, but when he called out the monkeys answered with helpful hoots and squeals, and he was soon standing at the bottom of the tree looking up into the friendly face of Monkey One, who had been sent down to find out what he wanted. George explained, using a mixture of sign language and grunts, and

Monkey One soon understood exactly what was required.

George returned to the Professor.

"I think it's going to work," he said. "They know what they have to do and I'm sure everything will be ready tomorrow morning."

The next morning, after another of the Professor's marvellous breakfasts, the two of them set off into the jungle. The Professor was thrilled that he would be able to see the home tree of the Congo Stripys and had brought his camera and notebooks with him. George was sure that the monkeys would not mind being studied by the Professor, and just to make sure that everything would be all right he had brought at least fifty bananas with him. This meant that there would be at least half a banana for each monkey.

Monkey One came out to meet them. He shook hands with the Professor and did not appear to mind the camera or the notebook in the least. He seemed keen to show them something, and so they did not go straight to the tree, but walked a short distance along a little path that wound further into the jungle.

Monkey One stopped and pointed off the path.

"They've done it," said George. "Look, they've collected everything we need."

"Indeed they have," said the Professor, noting something down in his notebook. "Everything's there."

And it was. There was a large pile of Congo Nuts – great, knobbly nuts almost the size of coconuts and twice as hard.

There was a neatly-stacked pile of bendy branches, all the right length and very springy. And there, exactly as they had hoped, were long lengths of thin vine, all neatly wound and ready for use.

"Now," said the Professor to George. "Can you get your monkey friend over here to call together ten of his best monkeys?"

George tapped Monkey One on the shoulder and, using the sign language which seemed to work so well, passed on the message that ten bright monkeys were needed. Monkey One seemed to understand immediately, and scampered off back to the tree. Soon he was back with ten fine-looking Congo Stripys, all smiling and ready for whatever it was that was to be asked of them.

George did the explaining, while the Professor took photographs and scribbled notes in his notebook.

"The plan is this," said George, in signs. "These horrid gorillas need to be taught a lesson. We're going to make traps all around your tree. When the gorillas come, they're going to get the fright of their lives and this should make them leave you in peace. Any questions?"

There were none. The monkeys all nodded wisely. They were keen to start and were delighted when George started handing out the vines and springy branches and the other bits and pieces which were needed to construct the traps. Then, all under the close supervision of George and Monkey One, they set to work preparing their little surprise.

It was hard work, and it was four or five hours before everything was ready. Monkey One was beginning to look worried, and from time to time glanced at his wrist, as if he were looking at a watch (which he did not have, of course).

"He's afraid the gorillas are going to arrive at any moment," George explained to the Professor.

Just as George spoke, Monkey One gave a screech of alarm.

"He's heard something," said the Professor, making a quick note in his notebook.

What Monkey One had heard was a distant roaring sound, and in a moment or two they all heard it. It was the sound of the gorillas, and it was getting closer with each moment.

"Quick," said George, pointing to the monkeys' tree. "Up we go."

The monkeys helped the Professor, who was not a very good climber, and soon they were all far enough up the tree to be safe. The other monkeys, particularly those who lived on the lower branches, were all chattering with alarm and trying to hook up their tails so that they would be out of reach of the gorillas' great hands.

"I hope it works," whispered the

Professor. "Otherwise we could be stuck up this tree for ever."

"It will work," said George. "Just you wait and see!"

Along the path came the group of four gorillas, beating their chests and roaring in a blood-curdling manner. They were looking forward to frightening the monkeys and to taking whatever food they could find, and so they were not particularly careful about where they put their feet.

And that, I'm afraid to say, was their undoing. As they approached the monkey tree, their great gorilla feet went straight into the nooses which the monkeys had so cunningly laid in the undergrowth. As the gorillas marched on, they pulled at the long strings of vine which connected the nooses to the nets of giant nuts which the monkeys had strung above the path. And as this happened, down came the nuts, every one of them finding its target – a gorilla's head!

As the nuts rained down on the gorillas, the great bullies let out howls of pain and charged towards the monkey tree, eager for revenge. But again they went straight into a trap, tripping over vines which had been strung across the jungle floor. These were connected to bent branches, which, now released, hurled fat parcels made out of banana leaves. Each of these parcels was filled with the slimiest and smelliest mud which the monkeys had been able to find. And each of these parcels landed exactly on target, covering the gorillas with mud!

The monkeys howled with mirth as the confused gorillas turned tail and ran back into the jungle. The younger monkeys swung from their tails, holding their stomachs in merriment, while the older ones, including Monkeys Two, Three and Four, wept with laughter.

After that, there was very little to do. The monkeys helped the Professor climb right up to the top of the tree, where they posed while he took photographs. Then, when everything had returned to normal, the bananas were handed out and everybody enjoyed a good feed.

That evening, back in their camp, the Professor and George discussed the day's events.

"Everything will be fine now," said the Professor. "We've taught the monkeys how to set up anti-gorilla traps, and so if the gorillas ever venture back – which I doubt – they'll learn their lesson all over again."

George was pleased that the monkeys would be safe. Now that everything was over, he wondered how they were going to spend their remaining days in the jungle. It could be rather dull, he thought, sitting on the edge of the river with nothing very much to do.

But he was wrong. Life in the jungle is never dull – as George was shortly to discover!

Chapter 7

The Monkeys Repay a Favour

Among the supplies which the Professor
had brought with him was an inflatable
boat. This he blew up the next morning
and announced to George that he was
going to row over to a tiny island in the
middle of the river. There were one or
two trees on this island – that's all there
was room for – and the Professor wanted

to see if there was any sign of monkey life.

George helped the Professor into the boat and gave it a push to set it on its way. Then he sat back and watched as the Professor rowed the little boat over the broad expanse of water towards the island.

The Professor had almost reached the island when George noticed that something was wrong. The boat, which was not very big anyway, seemed to be getting smaller.

"Is there anything wrong?" George shouted out across the water.

The Professor's reply was faint, but George was just able to make it out.

"A puncture!" shouted the Professor. "The boat's deflating!"

The Professor just made it to the island. With a last hiss, the inflatable boat collapsed and disappeared under the surface of the water.

"At least you're safe on dry land," shouted George. "I'll rescue you."

"How?" shouted the Professor.

George had no idea. But he did not want the Professor to become too alarmed, and so he called out, "I'll think of something. Don't you worry."

George sat down and thought. He could try to build a raft out of logs and sail that across to the island. That would take a long time, however, and he was not sure if he had anything with which to cut the logs. Or he could throw a rope across, and drag the Professor back through the water. But the problem with that was that they did not have a very long rope and. . . And!

George leaped to his feet as he thought of the other reason why this would not work. The crocodiles! The river was full of crocodiles, who even at that very moment might be watching what was going on with great interest.

Which they were. As George stood up and looked back at the island, he saw two dark shapes in the water, slowly circling the tiny island. Soon afterwards these shapes were joined by a third, and then a fourth. And there was no doubt what these shapes were, and what they were planning to do.

The Professor had seen them too.

"Crocodiles!" he shouted. "I'm surrounded by crocodiles!"

The crocodiles were getting closer now and as George watched in horror, one of them started to clamber up on to the island, directly behind the place where the Professor was standing.

"Look out!" shouted George, waving his arms up and down to attract the Professor's attention. "Look out behind you!"

The Professor spun round. The great crocodile was now very close to him, its eyes fixed intently on what it thought would be its next meal. With a yell of alarm, the Professor dashed towards the closest of the island's two trees and clambered up on to a branch.

He was just in time. The crocodile lurched towards him and snapped its great jaws in anger. It had hoped to get the Professor's leg, but succeeded only in getting his boot, which it munched contentedly. Then it settled down at the bottom of the tree, and was soon joined by its three friends, all looking hungrily up at the tree. They could wait. Crocodiles have plenty of time and sooner or later their meal would have to come down out of the tree. Or, if it didn't, sooner or later it would fall asleep, and would come tumbling down into their welcoming jaws.

George watched in horror. If only he could fetch help, but how could he do that in the middle of the jungle when there was nobody around for miles. Or was there? Suddenly he remembered. He had plenty of friends in this jungle – at least a hundred of them!

Without wasting any more time, George ran back towards the jungle.

Shouting at the top of his voice, he made his way towards the monkey tree, where Monkey One was waiting anxiously to find out what all the noise was about.

"Crocodiles!" gasped George, making a jaw-snapping sign with his hands. "They've surrounded the Professor!"

Monkey One seemed to understand.

Looking up into the tree, he let out an ear-piercing whistle and the ten fine monkeys who had helped set up the traps soon came swinging down to join them. Then, with George and Monkey One at their head, the whole troop rushed back towards the river.

Standing on the bank of the river with George, the monkeys were immediately able to see what the problem was. There were the crocodiles at the bottom of the tree, and there was the Professor halfway up.

Monkey One scratched his head. Then he turned to the others and uttered a string of excited squeaks. George had no idea what they were talking about, but it seemed as if Monkey One had had an idea.

The next thing that happened quite astonished George. Monkey One and his friends dashed off and scampered up a tall tree on the edge of the river. Then, after a few moments in the dense branches of the tree, a great length of vine suddenly dropped from the foliage. And at the end of the vine was Monkey

One himself, swinging backwards and forwards to gather momentum.

George had been puzzled at first, but now he could see exactly what was happening. Monkey One was swinging out over the river, further and further, until he was almost reaching the island.

George now knew what he had to do.

"Grab the rope!" he shouted to the Professor. "Grab it and swing back to shore!"

The Professor seemed to be flustered. But as the great vine came swinging back towards him, with Monkey One dangling at its end, he reached out and grabbed it.

Then, with as much of a push as he could manage, he launched himself – and Monkey One – from the tree.

The crocodiles had just noticed what was happening, and they all leaped up, jaws snapping furiously, to try to stop the Professor's escape. But they could not quite make it, although one of them succeeded in tearing off a tiny piece of fur from the tip of Monkey One's tail.

Out over the river swung the Professor and Monkey One. When the vine reached the edge, it was seized by the ten strong monkeys who were standing by, and after that the Professor and Monkey One slid to the ground.

"Thank you!" said the Professor, patting Monkey One on the back. "You've just saved my life."

Monkey One smiled. Monkeys always

like to repay a favour, and he was pleased that he had had the chance to help. The Professor had helped them, and now they had helped him. It was as simple as that.

The following day the plane returned. It almost missed the landing-strip, though, as the pilot could not see it very clearly. It was only when he saw the black-and-white flashes of a hundred Congo Stripys jumping up and down at the edge of the strip to attract his attention that he realized where he was.

The Professor and George loaded the plane, ably assisted by a number of helpful monkeys. Then they strapped themselves into their seats and the pilot started the engine.

"Goodbye!" George called out from the window. "We'll come back to see you soon!"

The monkeys, who had seemed a little sad to be seeing off their friends, were cheered up by this and waved goodbye happily enough. Then they went back to the edge of the jungle and watched as the plane sped along the landing strip and rose up into the air.

Soon it was no more than a spot in the sky and the monkeys all trooped back to their tree and to a meal of the delicious bananas which George and the Professor had so thoughtfully left them.

And high up in the air, as the plane climbed into the clouds and they settled down for the flight, George found a large leaf which had been tucked into the cabin by some unknown hand.

"Look," he said to the Professor. "It's a note from the monkeys."

They looked hard at the scribbled marks which had been etched on the leaf.

"What does it say?" asked George. "Is it monkey writing?"

The Professor smiled. "It is," he said. "And I think it just says, Thank you."